Where are my Shoes?

First published in 2003 by
Franklin Watts
96 Leonard Street
London
EC2A 4XD

Franklin Watts Australia
45–51 Huntley Street
Alexandria
NSW 2015

Text © Karen Wallace 2003
Illustration © Deborah Allwright 2003

A CIP catalogue record for this book is available
from the British Library.

ISBN 0 7496 5304 3 (hbk)
ISBN 0 7496 5368 X (pbk)

Series Editor: Jackie Hamley
Series Advisors: Dr Barrie Wade, Dr Hilary Minns
Design: Peter Scoulding

Printed in Hong Kong / China

To Glenn, from KW

Where are my Shoes?

Written by
Karen Wallace

Illustrated by
Deborah Allwright

W
FRANKLIN WATTS
LONDON•SYDNEY

Karen Wallace
"I love writing funny books so I can laugh at my own jokes. I wish I'd had a pair of shoes like Jack's when I was younger!"

Deborah Allwright
"I'm always working towards making my shoe collection even bigger!"

Jack is cross. "Where are my shoes?"

Are they under the bed?

8

No, but here is a wand!

Are they behind
the door?

11

No, but here is a cloak!

Are they on the table?

No, but here is a top hat!

"Where are your shoes?" shouts Mum.

20

Abracadabra!

"Here are my shoes!"
cries Jack.

22

Notes for parents and teachers

READING CORNER has been structured to provide maximum support for new readers. The stories may be used by adults for sharing with young children. Primarily, however, the stories are designed for newly independent readers, whether they are reading these books in bed at night, or in the reading corner at school or in the library.

Starting to read alone can be a daunting prospect. READING CORNER helps by providing visual support and repeating words and phrases, while making reading enjoyable. These books will develop confidence in the new reader, and encourage a love of reading that will last a lifetime!

If you are reading this book with a child, here are a few tips:

1. Make reading fun! Choose a time to read when you and the child are relaxed and have time to share the story.

2. Encourage children to reread the story, and to retell the story in their own words, using the illustrations to remind them what has happened.

3. Give praise! Remember that small mistakes need not always be corrected.

READING CORNER covers three grades of early reading ability, with three levels at each grade. Each level has a certain number of words per story, indicated by the number of bars on the spine of the book, to allow you to choose the right book for a young reader:

GRADE 1	GRADE 2	GRADE 3
50 words	130 words	250 words
70 words	160 words	350 words
100 words	200 words	450 words